To our mothers

CIP Data is available.

First published in the United States 1998
by Dutton Children's Books,
a member of Penguin Putnam Inc.
375 Hudson Street, New York, New York 10014
Originally published in Great Britain 1997 by Andersen Press Ltd., London
Typography by Ellen M. Lucaire
Printed in Italy
First American Edition
ISBN 0-525-45947-2
2 4 6 8 10 9 7 5 3 1

Baba Yaga & the Wise Doll

A TRADITIONAL RUSSIAN FOLKTALE

RETOLD BY Hiawyn Oram • ILLUSTRATED BY Ruth Brown

Dutton Children's Books ✦ New York

Once there was a witch called Baba Yaga.

"You are truly terrifying," her trusty Toads told her.

"I hope so," said Baba Yaga. "That's what I'm here for!"

One day Baba Yaga looked into her
Many-Ways mirror and saw what she saw:
Too Nice Child, Horrid Child, and Very Horrid Child.
"And I can see who will be visiting me in the very near
future," she cackled.

Even as Baba Yaga was cackling to herself, Horrid and Very
Horrid began to push Too Nice out of the house. "We don't want
you around," they said. "You're too nice. Go away—you can't play with us."

"I know you don't like me," said Too Nice. "But I can't always be alone.
What shall I do?"

"Go into the forest!" said Horrid.

"Yes," said Very Horrid with a crafty wink. "And visit Baba Yaga.

Bring us back one of her Toads in a jeweled jacket and diamond collar.
If you do that, we might play with you."

So Too Nice went out into the forest. She was all alone, except for her one dearest possession. It was a doll, given to her by her mother before she died.

"Now what?" Too Nice asked the Doll. "It's unbearable to stay and it's unbearable to go."

"No one can stay and go at the same time," said the Doll. "Put me in your pocket, listen to my advice whenever I have any, and let's be off."

So off went Too Nice with the Doll deep in her pocket. And, deep in the forest, Baba Yaga saw her coming.

Baba Yaga pulled her nose down and her chin up until they met in a terrifying crescent. She called to her side Broom, Cauldron, and all her Toads. She told House to unfold its scaly chicken legs and take them to meet the advancing child.

When Too Nice saw the House running toward her and Baba Yaga peering out from a chimney top, her legs turned to jelly.

"I can't do this," she said.

"Oh yes, you can," said the Doll from her pocket. "Just go right up and knock, and all will be well."

So Too Nice went up to the House.

"Yes?" squawked Baba Yaga in a voice like a rusty door. "And what do you want, little girl? Oh, never mind!" she sneered. "Nothing is for nothing. You want something, you work for it."

Then Baba Yaga waved at a mountain of dishes and a hill of dirty laundry. "Do it all by morning, or Cauldron will cook you."

Immediately Too Nice set to scrubbing and washing and ironing. But as midnight passed, she began to tremble.

"I'm cooked," she said to the Doll. "I can't do it."

"Yes, you can," said the Doll from her pocket. "You could do it in your sleep. In fact, sleep now, and all will be well."

So Too Nice curled up by the fire while the Doll finished the work.

In the morning, when the household woke up, Baba Yaga
saw the work all done and was impressed. But she didn't show it.
Instead she waved at a pile of dirt in the yard.

"In that pile," she wheezed, "is an equal amount of dirt
and poppy seeds. Separate them by this evening or my Toads
will taste you."

Immediately Too Nice got down to work. But as the sun
started to drop in the sky, she began to quiver and shake.

"I'm tidbits for Toads," Too Nice said, trembling. "I can't do this. Not in one day. Not in a thousand days."

"Yes, you can," said the Doll in her pocket. "You can do it with your eyes closed and your hands tied. In fact, shut your eyes for a while, and you'll see, all will be well."

So Too Nice sat down in the shade and shut her eyes while the Doll did the work.

When the household returned from the forest
at the end of the day, Baba Yaga was impressed.
But she didn't show it. Instead she waved Too Nice
toward the larder.

"In there is a heap of food. Lay it out for our
supper, then join us at the table."

And when the food was laid out and they were
all at the table, Baba Yaga's eyes glowed like hot coals.

"Now answer me correctly, or you'll be my first course.
What was it you came for?"

Immediately Too Nice opened her mouth to say,
"A Toad for Horrid and Too Horrid."

But she felt the Doll jumping up and down in
her pocket and answered instead, "To get a good scare,
of course, because that's what you're here for."

This time Baba Yaga showed she was impressed. She leaped onto the table and danced, in turn, with Broom, Cauldron, and Toads.

"That's the right answer, Little Wise One Beyond Your Years! How did you come to be so wise and pass all my tests?"

"Hmm," said Too Nice, feeling the Doll in her pocket. "By a gift from my mother."

"Well, gifts beget gifts!" cackled Baba Yaga.
And so she presented Too Nice with one of her Toads—
in a pearl-encrusted jacket, a diamond collar, and a long
emerald leash.

And when Too Nice led the Toad back to Horrid
and Very Horrid, he wasted no time. **ONE! TWO!**

He gobbled them up, then quietly hopped back to the forest.
And Too Nice—not surprisingly after all she'd been through—
stopped being too nice and became . . . well . . . Just About Right.

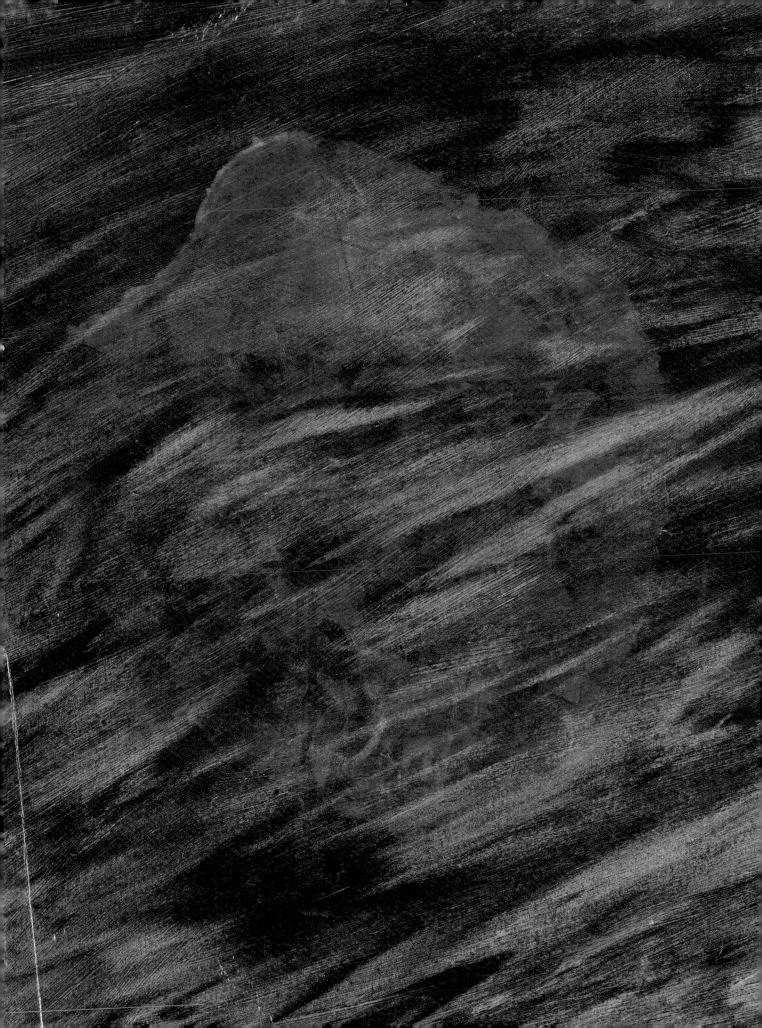